With grateful acknowledgment to:

God's direction and guidance in my life, it's so good to know you're always there.
Thank you

Wayne J. Lamarre, the illustrator,
There is not enough room on this page to give you all the thanks and praise you deserve
for the way you brought Billy's world to life.   You are a true credit to the art world and a true friend
in our world. You are the best! Thank you Wayne.

My technical crew, Danny Sletten, and Jim Cheeseman, for all their involvement and knowledge in the field
of graphic design. You guys are great, Thank you.

To Paul Poisson, my Production Artist for the attention and unconditional effort you gave to this project. It was
simply amazing the way you took everything and put it all together. You are fantastic!
Thank you Paul.

To my family members for all their involvement and support, but most of all, for their unconditional love.

To my cousin, Kristen Maclean, "My little miss kris!" This story was inspired by a poem I wrote for her
when she was involved with competitive figure skating.
Kristen, you will always be a winner in whatever you do.
Thank you Kristen.

To my wonderful Gilda,
for being right there with me through everything, and giving me the strength and determination
for all my accomplishments. Together we can do anything.
I love you Gillie.

I would like to dedicate this book to children everywhere.   For the way they pour their
little hearts out into everything they do, no matter what the outcome,
these are the real winners.
Now get ready because,
It's time to
BEELIEVE.

Peter Thomas

THE ADVENTURES OF BILLY BEE™

"WINNING"

BY PETER THOMAS
ILLUSTRATED BY WAYNE J. LAMARRE

Published by:
Billy Bee Productions, Inc.
455 Boston Road
Billerica, MA 01821

Library of Congress Catalog Card Number: 95-67530
Library of Congress Cataloging-in-Publication Data
Main entry under title:
The Adventures of Billy Bee
Subtitle: Winning
Children's Fiction/Sports/Winning/Self Belief
Author, Peter Thomas
First Edition   10 9 8 7 6 5 4 3 2 1

ISBN 1-886919-02-X

**Billy Bee was at school one day
and went out to the playground.
He sat and watched the football game
where no one was around.**

Billy dreamed he was the star,
while he sat and watched the game,
his team would win because of him
and the crowd would scream his name.

Wanda Worm was also watching
as the girls were cheering on the side.
"Oh if I had arms and legs,
I could cheer as well!" she cried.

"I would jump the highest,
and the crowd would hear me scream.
I would be the best cheerleader."
This was Wanda's dream.

**Then suddenly and all at once,
someone screamed in pain.
Timmy Termite hurt himself
and they had to stop the game.**

The coach ran over quickly,
to see just what was wrong.
Timmy had just hurt his leg,
now the game could not go on.

7

The coach said, "Can another play?
That would be alright with me."
Then someone yelled, "Look over there,
I see it's Billy Bee!"

"Oh Billy will you play with us
and help our team to win?"
Billy thought about his dreams
and said, "Yes, let the game begin!"

So then the game continued,
and Doug threw out a pass,
but it went over Billy's head,
and landed in the grass.

Then the crowd began to laugh,
when Billy didn't catch the ball,
but he told Doug to throw it lower,
because he was not that tall.

11

So the game went on again,
and they all began to play.
Doug threw the ball to Cecil
but Billy Bee got in the way.

"Oh Billy Bee, we thought you said
that you could play this game,
that you would be so very good,
the crowd would scream your name."

But the crowd was screaming nothing.
The girls weren't cheering on the side,
and Billy felt so very bad,
he walked away and cried.

14

With tear drops in his eyes,
he went where no one else could see;
past the playground, up to school,
but Wanda was cheering Billy Bee!

"BILLY BEE, BILLY BEE,
YOU'LL BE GOOD THE CROWD WILL SEE,
BILLY BEE, BILLY BEE,
THEY ALL WILL HEAR YOUR NAME FROM ME!"

"Oh Wanda Worm, you're very nice,
but how can you cheer my name?
I thought I would be very good,
but I cannot play this game."

"Oh Billy, you have arms and legs,
to run and catch the ball.
It doesn't matter if you're good or not,
just do your best, that's all."

"I have no arms or legs, Billy.
This has always been my dream,
but I have a voice to call your name,
so the crowd will hear me scream."

**When Billy Bee heard Wanda Worm
and what she had to say,
he felt so good about himself,
that he decided he would play.**

So Billy went back and told the team,
"Let's try our best to win this game."
"Oh Billy, we're almost out of time
and the score is still the same."

21

**Then, Billy told Doug to throw the ball
up in the air so high,
and he would do his very best
to catch the ball, he'd try.**

**So the game went on just one last time,
and Doug with all his might,
threw the ball so high up in the air,
it flew higher than a kite.**

**Billy Bee was running,
running so very fast.
He ran by all the players.
Yes, everyone he passed.**

The coach and Timmy Termite,
were both cheering on the side,
because no one could catch Billy Bee,
how ever hard they tried.

**When Billy looked up to catch the ball,
the sun was there instead.
It was so strong he could not see,
and that's when Billy said:**

26

"A BIZZ, A BUZZ, A BEEZ, A BAMM
I'M BILLY BEE, I AM, I AM!
I CAN DO ANYTHING, I KNOW I CAN,
BECAUSE I'M BILLY BEE, I AM, I AM!"

**Then Billy Bee held up his arms,
because he was not that tall.
He stood up on his tippy toes,
and then he caught the ball!**

The clock ran out, his teammates cheered,
because Billy won the game.
The crowd was clapping loudly,
and screaming Billy's name!

**So the players picked up Billy Bee,
and the cheerleaders on the side,
went and picked up Wanda Worm.
"You two are great," they cried.**

**When Wanda Worm and Billy Bee
were way up high they met,
and Wanda Worm told Billy Bee,
"This you must never, ever, forget:"**

"When the games all begin, and you start to perform,
and the crowd starts to clap loud and shout,
just believe in yourself, and do the best that you can,
because that is what winning's about!"